BIBLE
FOOD
FUN

A STEP-BY-STEP
COOKBOOK

LESLEY WRIGHT

TYNDALE HOUSE PUBLISHERS, INC.
Wheaton, Illinois

A DORLING KINDERSLEY BOOK

For Danni

Editor Jane Yorke
Art Editor Rachel Salter
Senior Managing Editor
Sarah Phillips
Deputy Art Director
Mark Richards
DTP Designer Megan Clayton
Production Linda Dare
Jacket Design Rachel Salter
U.S. Editor Claudia Volkman

Photography by James Jackson
Illustrations by Julie Downing

Published in the United States by
Tyndale House Publishers, Inc.
351 Executive Drive
Carol Steam, Illinois 60188

Visit Tyndale's exciting Web site at
www.tyndale.com

Copyright © 2000 Dorling Kindersley
Limited, London

2 4 6 8 10 9 7 5 3 1

ISBN: 0-8423-3685-0

Color reproduction by
Colourscan, Singapore
Printed and bound in China by L Rex

DK would like to thank the following people
for their help in the making of this book:
Paul Bailey for photography assistance,
Lauren Banyard and Karen Beckwith
for hand-modeling. Special thanks to
Kathy Bolton, food technologist.

COOK'S SAFETY RULES

Cooking is lots of fun, but it's important to read these safety rules before you begin working in the kitchen.

1 Always wash your hands before preparing food. Protect your clothes with an apron, roll up your sleeves, and tie long hair back out of the way.

2 Read through your chosen recipe carefully. Gather together all the cooking utensils you will need. Prepare a clean work area.

3 Collect all the listed ingredients together. Weigh the dry ingredients and measure the liquid ingredients using a measuring cup.

4 Never start cooking without an adult being present. Whenever you see this oven mitt safety symbol in a recipe, be extra careful and ask an adult for help.

5 Always ask an adult to turn the oven on and off for you. Never handle hot pans, baking trays, or liquids without adult help. Wear oven mitts whenever you need to pick up hot, or even warm, things.

6 When cooking on the stove, keep pan handles turned to the side so that you cannot knock them over.

7 When stirring hot food in a pan on the stove, always hold the pan handle firmly as you work.

8 Be very careful when using sharp knives. Keep the knife blade pointing downward and away from you and use a cutting board. Always prepare meat on a separate board not used with other foods.

9 Make sure that your hands are dry when plugging in and using electric appliances.

10 Use a cloth to wipe up any spills as you go along. Wash your utensils when you have finished cooking and clean up any mess.

CONTENTS

You will need

Baking sheet • Rolling pin • Sharp knife
Can opener • Mixing bowl • Fork
Butter knife • Cutting board
Cheese grater • Pastry brush

Ingredients for 1 large pizza

 10 oz (295 g) pkg. pizza crust mix – or frozen pizza crust

 2 tablespoons tomato purée

 14¹/₂ oz (400 g) can diced tomatoes

1 teaspoon Italian seasoning

 1 tablespoon cooking oil

¹/₂ cup (115 g) grated cheddar cheese

Salt and pepper for seasoning

Flour for dusting the work surface

Toppings

 ¹/₂ cup (115 g) chopped ham

1 zucchini

 1 small can sweet corn

4 cherry tomatoes

1 green pepper

1 black olive for decoration

BIG FISH PIZZA

You can make a scrumptious pizza by following this quick and easy recipe. Turn the page to see the finished fishy dish.

Jonah and the big fish
Jonah was a person who learned a hard lesson. When God asked him to do something, Jonah thought it would be too difficult and ran away to sea. He was thrown overboard during a big storm. Then a wonderful thing happened. God sent a huge fish to rescue Jonah. Find out how this fishy tale ends by reading Jonah 1-2.

Making the pizza

1 Preheat the oven to 425°F/ 220°C. Dust the work surface with flour. Roll out the pizza crust dough into a large oval shape.

2 Use a butter knife to cut out a large fish shape, as shown. Place the pizza crust on a greased baking sheet and set aside.

3 Open the cans of sweet corn and tomatoes and drain well. Mix the tomatoes in a bowl with the herbs and salt and pepper.

4 Next wash the zucchini, tomatoes, and green pepper. Use a sharp knife to cut them into thin slices for the fish scales.

5 Use a butter knife to spread the tomato purée all over the pizza crust. Then cover with the mixture of tomato and herbs.

6 Grate the cheddar cheese and sprinkle it evenly over the pizza crust. Put an extra layer of cheese on the fish's head and tail.

Decorating the pizza

1 Decorate your big fish pizza with the sweet corn, chopped ham, and sliced toppings in curved rows to look like fish scales.

2 Brush the scales lightly with oil and place your pizza in the oven. Bake for about 30–35 minutes or follow package instructions.

Fishy meal

Decorate your big fish pizza with all your favorite tasty toppings.

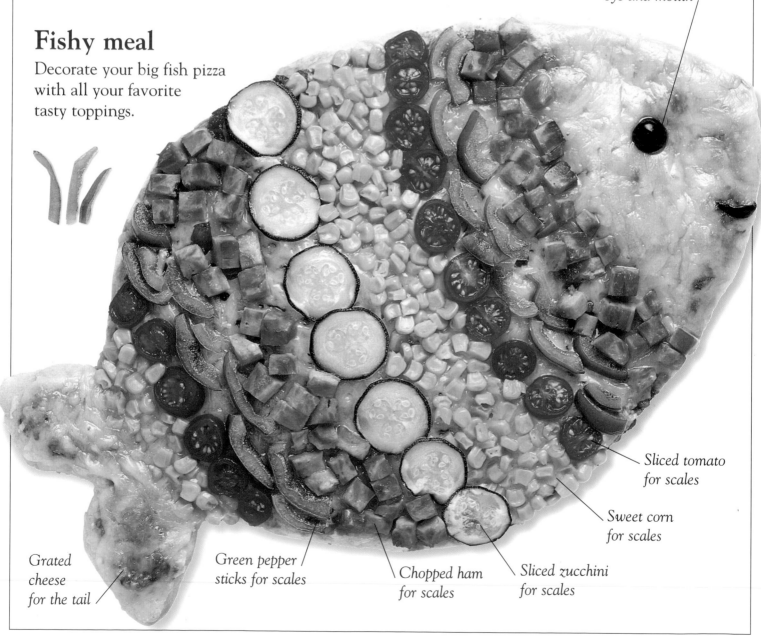

Olive slices for the eye and mouth

Sliced tomato for scales

Sweet corn for scales

Grated cheese for the tail

Green pepper sticks for scales

Chopped ham for scales

Sliced zucchini for scales

DANIEL'S CHEESY LIONS

I f you're roaring with hunger, try baking these cheesy lion scones. Follow the steps below and on the next page and make a snacktime feast that will satisfy all appetites.

Daniel in the lions' den
Daniel was a good man who trusted in God. He continued to pray even after King Darius passed a law to stop people from worshiping God.

You will need

2¹/₂ in (6 cm) round cookie cutter
Baking sheet • Mixing bowl
Strainer • Rolling pin • Scissors
Cheese grater • Pastry brush
Sharp knife

Ingredients for 4 lion scones

1 cup (225 g) self-rising flour

1 teaspoon baking powder

Pinch of salt

¹/₂ teaspoon dry mustard

3 tablespoons (45 g) butter

¹/₂ cup (115 g) grated cheddar cheese

¹/₂ cup (150 ml) milk

4 black olives for decoration

Making the lions

1 Preheat the oven to 425°F/ 220°C. Sift the flour into a bowl. Add the baking power, dry mustard, and salt.

2 Grease and flour a baking sheet. Rub the butter into the flour with your fingertips until it looks like breadcrumbs.

Making the lions continued

3 Grate the cheese and mix into the bowl. Add enough milk to bind the mixture together and knead it into a ball of dough.

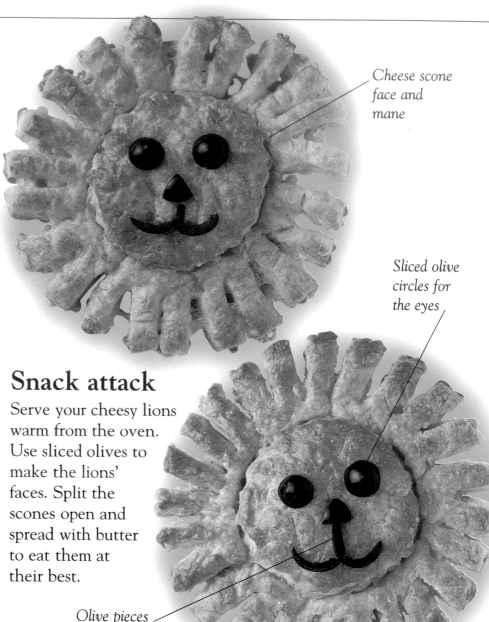

Cheese scone face and mane

Sliced olive circles for the eyes

Snack attack

Serve your cheesy lions warm from the oven. Use sliced olives to make the lions' faces. Split the scones open and spread with butter to eat them at their best.

Olive pieces for the nose and mouth

4 Next dust your work surface with some flour. Roll out the scone dough until it's about 1/2 in (1 cm) thick all over.

5 Cut out four circles for the lions' faces and put them far apart on the baking sheet. Knead together the rest of the dough.

6 Roll out the dough. Cut it into four strips 8 in (20 cm) long and 1 in (2.5 cm) wide. Snip all along one edge of each strip.

7 Carefully wrap the manes around the lions' faces. Gently press the dough together and spread out the manes.

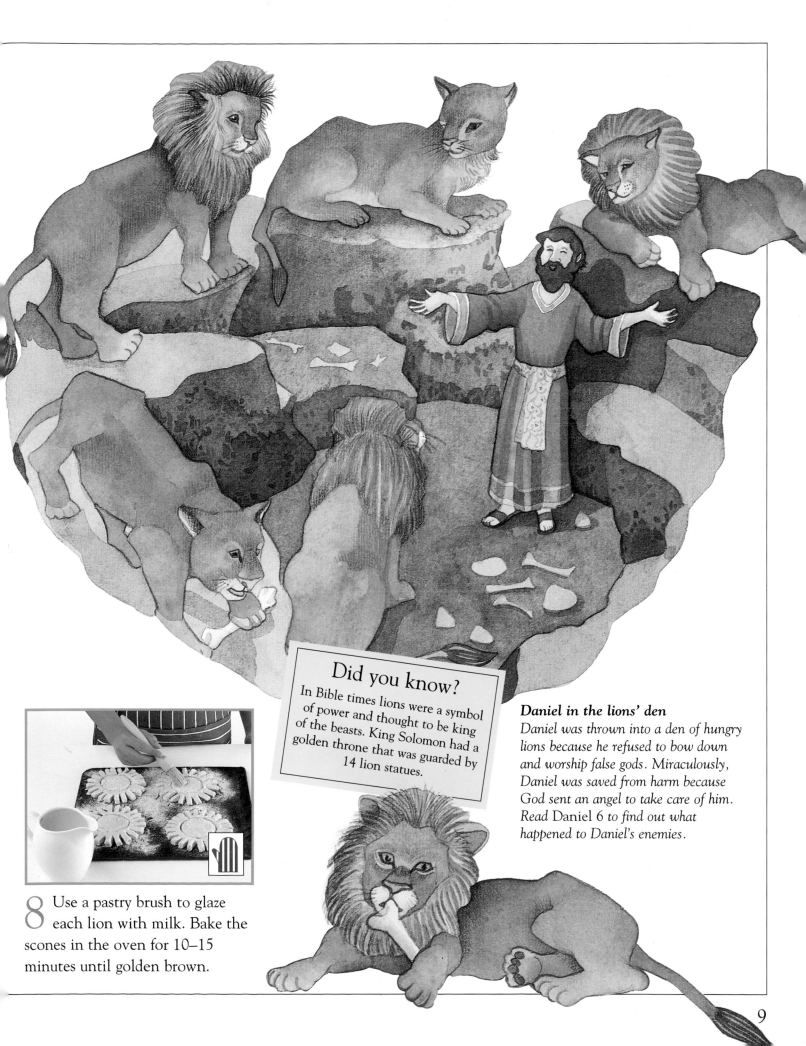

Daniel in the lions' den
Daniel was thrown into a den of hungry lions because he refused to bow down and worship false gods. Miraculously, Daniel was saved from harm because God sent an angel to take care of him. Read Daniel 6 to find out what happened to Daniel's enemies.

8 Use a pastry brush to glaze each lion with milk. Bake the scones in the oven for 10–15 minutes until golden brown.

DOUBLE-DECKER FISH FEAST

T his yummy tuna club sandwich can be fixed in a flash and will fill you to the brim – who knows, there may even be some left over!

You will need

Can opener • Sharp knife
Cutting board • Butter knife
Fork • Small mixing bowl

Ingredients for 1 sandwich

3 thick slices whole wheat bread

3 oz (115 g) can tuna fish

1 tablespoon mayonnaise

Cucumber

Lettuce

1 tomato

1 tablespoon cream cheese

2 toothpicks

Did you know?

Most people ate fish in Bible times because meat was expensive. People didn't have refrigerators like we do today, so they kept fish from rotting by salting it and drying it in the sun.

Lots of hungry people

Jesus had been teaching the crowds all day, and the people were hungry. The disciples found one small boy with a lunch of five loaves and two small fish – nowhere near enough food to feed over 5,000 people. Jesus blessed the meal, and an amazing thing happened. When the disciples handed out the food, everyone was able to eat with plenty to spare. How many baskets of food were left over? Read Mark 6:30-44 to find out if you guessed right.

Making the sandwich

1 Open the can of tuna fish and drain it. Put the tuna in a bowl and use a fork to mix the fish with the mayonnaise.

2 Toast or grill the slices of bread and chop off the crusts. Shred some lettuce and cut the cucumber and tomato into slices.

3 Spread the bottom slice of toast with cream cheese. Add a layer of tomato and lettuce. Next add a second layer of toast.

4 Cover with a layer of tuna fish and mayonnaise mixture and cucumber. Top with the toast and hold it together with toothpicks.

Toasted bread

Toothpick

Sliced cucumber

Tuna fish and mayonnaise layer

Cream cheese layer

Shredded lettuce

Super sandwich

Cut your double-decker sandwich in half and enjoy your mouth-watering meal. Remember to remove the toothpicks before you take a bite.

Sliced tomato

EASTER BREAD CROSSES

You will need

Mixing bowl • Strainer • Sharp knife
Measuring cup • 2 baking sheets
Wooden spoon • Scissors
Pastry brush • Plastic wrap

Ingredients for 4 bread crosses

 $2\frac{1}{4}$ cups (340 g) all-purpose flour

1 cup (225 ml) warm, not hot, water

 1 teaspoon salt

1 tablespoon (15 g) butter

 $\frac{1}{2}$ package (2 level teaspoons) active dried yeast

2 tablespoons cooking oil

 Poppy seeds for decoration

Celebrate Easter by baking some special bread rolls. Follow these simple steps and find out how to shape your dough into delicious bread crosses. Turn over the page to see the finished baked bread.

Making the dough

1 Preheat the oven to 450°F/ 230°C. Grease and flour two baking sheets. Sift the flour, salt, and yeast into a bowl. Rub in the butter.

2 Make a well in the mixture and stir in the warm water to make a soft dough. Add more flour if it's too sticky, more water if it's too dry.

The first Easter

Jesus was nailed to a wooden cross beside two thieves. Before he died, Jesus asked God to forgive the people who plotted to kill him. One soldier who heard this said, "Truly, this is the Son of God." Jesus' body was laid in a tomb and sealed with a huge stone. But what happened three days later? Find out by reading Matthew 28.

3 Place the dough on a floured work surface. Fold the dough from top to bottom and firmly push your knuckles into the center.

4 Give the dough a quarter turn and knead it again as before. Repeat this process for about 5–10 minutes. Cut the dough into four.

5 Roll each piece of dough into an 11 in (28 cm) long roll. From one end, cut off a short piece measuring 4 in (10 cm).

6 Use scissors to snip a small wedge out of each piece. Place the pieces together on a baking sheet in the shape of a cross.

13

Baking the crosses

1 Brush the crosses with oil and sprinkle with poppy seeds. Cover with plastic wrap and leave the dough to rise in a warm place.

2 After about 15 minutes, bake the crosses in the oven for 15 minutes. Test your baked bread. It should sound hollow when tapped.

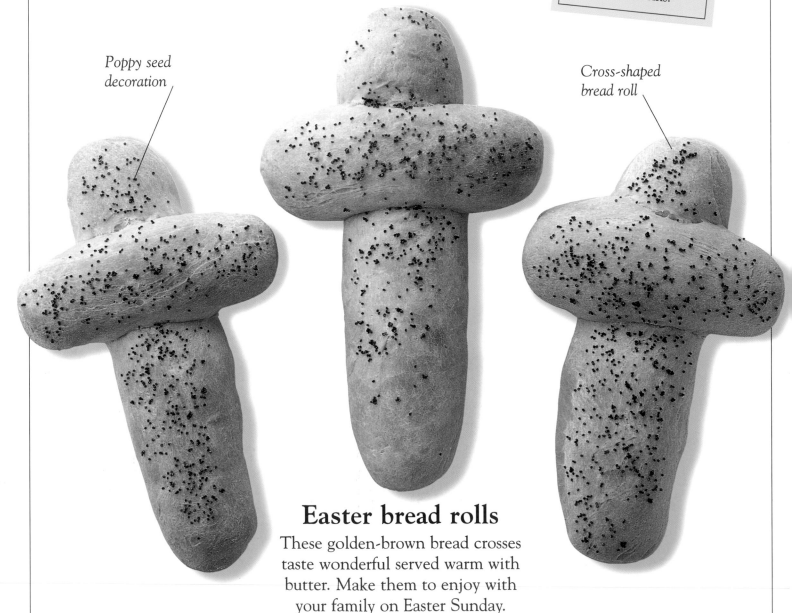

Poppy seed decoration

Cross-shaped bread roll

Easter bread rolls

These golden-brown bread crosses taste wonderful served warm with butter. Make them to enjoy with your family on Easter Sunday.

EVE'S APPLE CRUMBLE

This apple dessert has easy-to-follow steps and is deliciously tempting – treat yourself to a second helping!

You will need

8 or 9 in (22 cm) round pie plate
Sharp knife • Vegetable peeler
Cutting board • Wooden spoon
Saucepan • Lemon juicer
Cheese grater • Mixing bowl
Strainer • Large metal spoon

Ingredients

 $1^{1}/_{2}$ lb (675 g) cooking apples

1 tablespoon orange marmalade

 1 orange

$^{1}/_{2}$ teaspoon cinnamon

 $^{1}/_{2}$ cup (115 g) all-purpose flour

4 tablespoons (85 g) butter

 $^{1}/_{4}$ cup (55 g) rolled oats

$^{1}/_{4}$ cup (55 g) brown sugar

Butter for greasing

Adam and Eve
The first man and woman on earth were Adam and Eve. God gave them the beautiful Garden of Eden and told them to care for all the plants and animals that lived there. But God gave Adam and Eve one rule – he told them never to eat the fruit from one tree that grew in the garden.

Making the crumble

1 Preheat the oven to 375°F/ 190°C. Peel and core the apples, cut them into slices and place in the saucepan.

2 Grate the skin of an orange and set aside. Squeeze the juice of the orange and pour into the saucepan with the apple slices.

Making the crumble continued

3 Add the marmalade and cinnamon to the saucepan and cook gently on a low heat until the apples are soft.

4 Grease the pie plate with some butter. Spoon the apple mixture evenly into the pie plate and set aside.

5 Next, make the crumble topping. Sift the flour into a mixing bowl and stir in the grated orange zest.

6 Add the butter to the bowl. Mix the butter into the flour with your fingertips until it looks like fine bread crumbs.

7 Add the rolled oats and sugar to the bowl. Stir the crumble ingredients and mix well to make the crumble topping.

8 Sprinkle the crumble topping evenly over the apples and bake for about 30–35 minutes, until the topping is golden brown.

Apple delight

This hot fruit dessert is perfect for a cold winter's day. Serve your apple crumble straight from the oven topped with whipped cream or scoops of vanilla ice cream.

Adam and Eve

One day, Satan disguised himself as a talking snake and tempted Eve to eat the fruit from the forbidden tree. Eve shared the tasty fruit with Adam. Immediately, they both felt ashamed. What happened when God found out that Adam and Eve had disobeyed him? Read the rest of the story in Genesis 3.

Tangy apple filling

Crunchy crumble topping

NOAH'S ANIMALS

You will need

Mixing bowl • Rolling pin • Strainer
Wire cooling rack • Cutting board
1 in (2.5 cm) round cookie cutter
Whisk • Wooden spoon • Waxed paper

Ingredients for up to 30 candies

2 cups (340 g)
confectioners'
sugar

1 egg white

2–3 drops peppermint extract

2–3 drops lemon extract

2–3 drops yellow
food coloring

2–3 drops black
food coloring

This mouthwatering candy is very easy to make and needs no cooking at all! Which is your favorite – the peppermint zebras or the lemon leopards?

Noah's ark

God asked Noah, the one good man left in the world, to build a huge boat called an ark. He told Noah to fill the ark with a male and female pair of every kind of bird and animal. God wanted to save Noah and his family and all the animals before he sent a flood to destroy the world. After the Flood, which creature helped Noah to look for dry land? See how the story ends in Genesis 8.

Peppermint
zebra candy

Lemon
leopard
candy

Making the zebra candy

1 Place a sheet of waxed paper on a wire cooling rack. Whisk the egg white in a bowl until it's frothy, but not stiff.

2 Sift the confectioners' sugar into the bowl a little at a time. Keep stirring the mixture with a wooden spoon until it gets stiff.

3 Work the mixture into a soft ball with your fingers. Divide the icing into three balls: two large and one small.

4 Knead the peppermint extract into a large ball of icing. Roll it out on a work surface dusted with the sugar until it's ¼ in (5 mm) thick.

5 Knead the black food coloring into the small ball of icing. Roll out strips and lay them on the white icing. Save the leftover black icing.

6 Roll out the striped icing. Use the round cookie cutter to cut out the zebra candy. Lay them on waxed paper to dry out.

Making the leopard candy

1 Mix the lemon extract and yellow food coloring into the last ball of icing and roll it out. Add tiny balls of the saved black icing.

2 Roll out the icing again and use the cutter to cut out the spotted leopard candy. Leave the candy on the waxed paper to dry.

Spots and stripes

Arrange your candy on a plate to make a striped zebra face and a spotted leopard face. Invite your friends to take their pick of these delicious sweet creams.

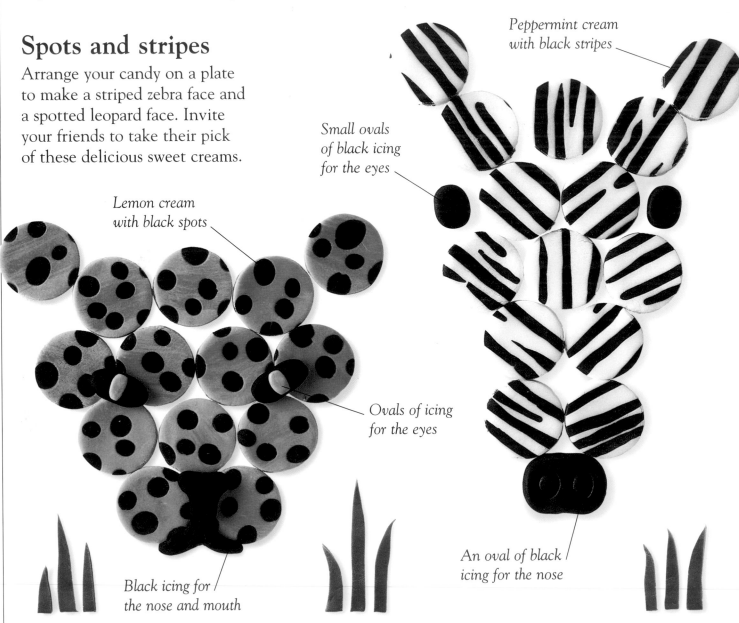

Lemon cream with black spots

Small ovals of black icing for the eyes

Peppermint cream with black stripes

Ovals of icing for the eyes

Black icing for the nose and mouth

An oval of black icing for the nose

ANGEL CAKES

These strawberry cupcakes are very quick to bake and they taste so divine, you'd think they were made in heaven!

You will need

Mixing bowl • Small bowl
Wooden spoon • Large spoon
2 muffin tins • 2 tablespoons
Sharp knife • Cutting board
Wire cooling rack • Strainer
12 paper bake cups • Fork

Ingredients for 12 cakes

1 cup (115 g)
self-rising flour

$^{1}/_{2}$ cup (115 g)
granulated sugar

$^{1}/_{4}$ cup (115 g)
butter

 2 eggs

1 teaspoon
baking powder

 2–3 drops
vanilla extract

For the fillings

6 strawberries

 1 cup (150 ml)
frozen whipped
topping, thawed

The birth of Jesus
God sent his messenger, the angel Gabriel, to tell a young woman called Mary that she was going to have a very special baby. Mary was engaged to be married to a carpenter called Joseph. The angel said that the baby was the Son of God, and that Mary and Joseph should name him Jesus.

Making the cakes

1 Preheat the oven to 400°F/ 200°C. Place the 12 paper bake cups into the muffin tins. Wash the strawberries and cut them in half.

2 Cream the butter and sugar together in a bowl with a wooden spoon. Keep beating until the mixture is light and fluffy.

Making the cakes continued

3 Beat the eggs in a small bowl with a fork. Add the eggs a little at a time and beat into the mixture. Add the vanilla extract.

4 Sift the baking powder and flour into the bowl, a little at a time. Gently fold the flour into the mixture with a large spoon.

5 Check that the cake mixture drops easily off the spoon. If it's too stiff, add a tablespoon of water and check the mixture again.

Did you know?
Angels are heavenly beings who carry God's messages between heaven and earth. Only two angels are named in the Bible. One is the angel Gabriel, God's messenger who appeared to Mary. The other is the warrior archangel Michael, who fought against Satan.

The birth of Jesus
One night out in the fields, some shepherds were keeping watch over their flocks of sheep. Suddenly, a shining angel appeared in the sky and spoke to the frightened shepherds. The angel told them the wonderful news that a Savior had been born in Bethlehem. When the shepherds went to worship the baby Jesus, where did they find him? Read about their visit in Luke 2:8-20.

6 Put a tablespoon of cake mixture into each bake cup. Place the muffin tins on the top rack of the oven and bake for 15 minutes.

7 Let the cakes cool. Use a knife to cut a thin slice off the top of each cake. Cut the circles in half to make wings.

8 Fill the hollows in the cakes with whipped cream and place the wings on either side of the cream. Top with half a strawberry.

Heavenly cakes

These delicious strawberry angel cakes just melt in the mouth. Enjoy them as a special afternoon snack.

Whipped cream filling

Juicy strawberry topping

Cake semicircles for the wings

Cupcake

JOSEPH'S SUNDAE BEST

You will need

Sundae glass • Ice-cream scoop
Sharp knife • Cutting board
Strainer • Can opener

Ingredients for 2 servings

 4 scoops
French vanilla
ice cream

 1/2 cup (115 g)
strawberries

 1/2 cup (115 g)
blueberries

2 kiwifruits

 1 small can
mandarin
orange slices

This colorful ice-cream treat is a fruity feast ready in minutes. Follow each simple step and let this delicious dessert brighten up your Sunday!

Making the sundae

1 Wash the fresh fruit. Peel and slice the kiwifruit. Remove the hulls from the strawberries and cut into quarters.

2 Drain the can of mandarin orange slices. Place a layer of blueberries in the bottom of each glass. Add a layer of oranges.

3 Next, fill the sundae glass with a layer of sliced kiwifruit, followed by a layer of chopped strawberries.

4 Add two scoops of vanilla ice cream. Finally, decorate with strawberries, blueberries, and a slice of kiwifruit.

Rainbow fruits

Make up your own sundae recipes using seasonal fruits and your favorite ice-cream flavors.

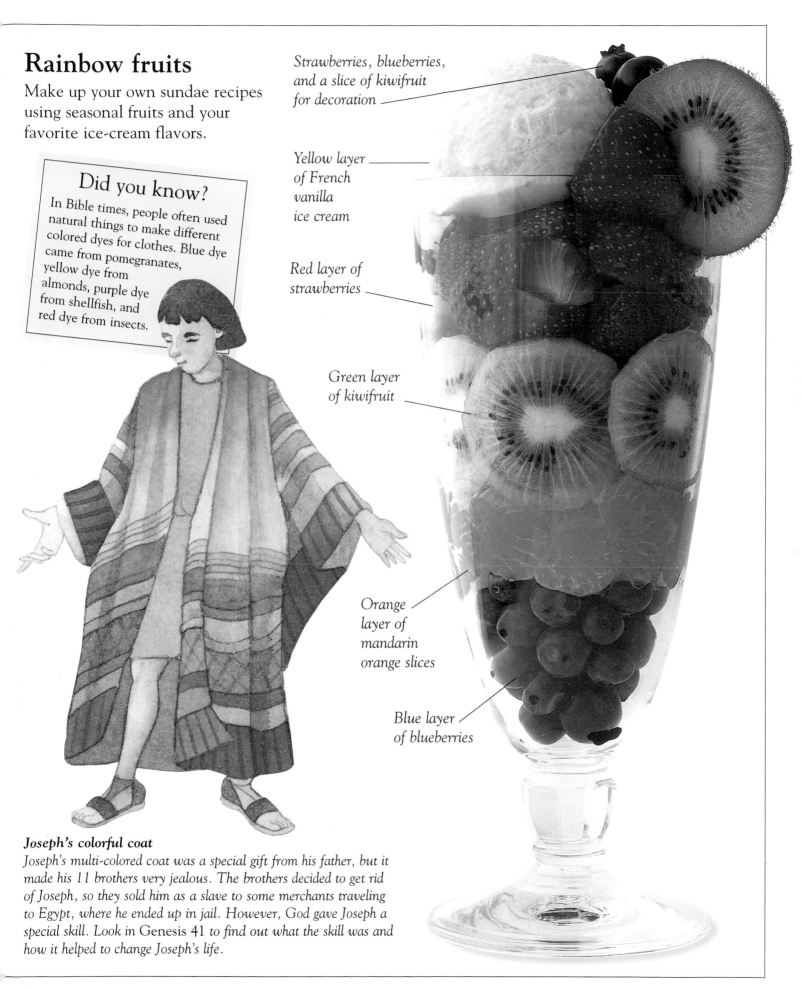

Strawberries, blueberries, and a slice of kiwifruit for decoration

Yellow layer of French vanilla ice cream

Red layer of strawberries

Green layer of kiwifruit

Orange layer of mandarin orange slices

Blue layer of blueberries

Joseph's colorful coat

Joseph's multi-colored coat was a special gift from his father, but it made his 11 brothers very jealous. The brothers decided to get rid of Joseph, so they sold him as a slave to some merchants traveling to Egypt, where he ended up in jail. However, God gave Joseph a special skill. Look in Genesis 41 to find out what the skill was and how it helped to change Joseph's life.

CHOCOLATE MOSES BASKETS

Try your hand at these crunchy chocolate treats. The little Moses figures are easy to make and taste as good as they look!

You will need

Saucepan • Small bowl • Fork
9 paper bake cups • Rolling pin
2 teaspoons • Muffin tin • Sharp knife
Cutting board • Toothpick

Ingredients for 9 cakes

3 large shredded wheat biscuits

6 oz (175 g) semisweet chocolate

8 oz (225 g) white fondant icing (found in specialty food shops)

2–3 drops each green, yellow, red, and blue food coloring

Did you know?

Moses was discovered in a basket made of papyrus reeds. The ancient Egyptians also used papyrus to make the first kind of paper. They wrote with pictures called hieroglyphs on this paper using reed brushes dipped in paints.

Moses in the bulrushes

In Egypt, Pharaoh gave the order for all the Israelite baby boys to be killed. One mother thought of a clever way to save her baby. She wove a basket out of dried reeds, placed her baby in the basket and hid him among the bulrushes in the River Nile. When Pharaoh's daughter came down to the river to bathe, she discovered the baby and decided to adopt him as her son. Who do you think the princess paid to look after the baby for her? Find out in Exodus 2.

Making the baskets

1 Break the chocolate into a bowl. Place the bowl in a saucepan of water over a low heat. Stir until the chocolate melts.

2 Break the shredded wheat biscuits into small pieces. Add them to the chocolate and stir until the wheat is well-coated.

3 Put the bake cups in the muffin tin. Spoon some mixture into each cup. Use the back of a spoon to make a hollow in each basket.

4 Cut the icing into four. Roll out two pieces and cut into 18 parts. Form nine simple baby shapes and nine circles for shawls.

5 Cut the last two pieces of icing in half. Mix food coloring into each piece. Roll out the green icing. Add stripes of colored icing.

6 Use a rolling pin to flatten the striped icing. Cut out nine blankets and place over the babies in the chocolate baskets.

Baby's eyes made with a toothpick

Stripes of red, blue, green, and yellow icing for the blanket

White icing shawl wrapped around baby Moses

Chocolate-covered shredded wheat for the basket

Chocolate treats

These pretty chocolate Moses baskets are perfect for serving at a party. Let the baskets harden in a cool place by storing them in an airtight container.

SQUASHED FLY SHORTBREAD

This tasty shortbread is very easy to bake – just follow the simple recipe. Invite your friends to take a bite, but tell them to watch out for the flies!

You will need

Mixing bowl • Sharp knife • Strainer
8 in (20 cm) round cake pan • Fork
Wire cooling rack • Wooden spoon

Ingredients for 8 servings

 $^1/_2$ cup (85 g) all-purpose flour

$^1/_4$ cup (85 g) cornmeal

 4 tablespoons (115 g) butter

$^1/_4$ cup (55 g) granulated sugar

$^1/_4$ cup (55 g) raisins

Granulated sugar for sprinkling

The plagues of Egypt
God called Moses to lead his people out of Egypt. Moses asked Pharaoh many times to let God's people go, but Pharaoh wouldn't listen. So God sent ten terrible plagues to make Pharaoh change his mind. How many plagues can you name? Check your answers in Exodus 7-11.

Making the shortbread

1 Set the oven to 350°F/ 180°C. Cream the butter and sugar together with a wooden spoon until light and fluffy.

2 Sift the flour and cornmeal into the bowl. Add the raisins and knead the mixture into a soft dough.

3 Grease and flour the cake pan. Press the dough firmly into the pan and prick all over with a fork. Bake for 40–45 minutes.

4 Once the shortbread is baked, mark the cutting lines with a knife and let cool. Finally, sprinkle the shortbread with sugar.

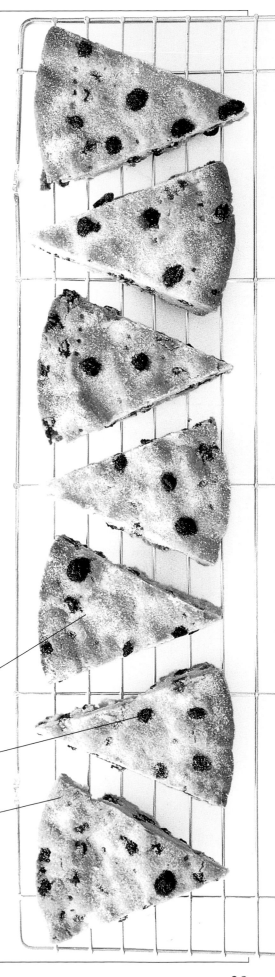

Granulated sugar topping

"Squashed fly" raisins

Shortbread

Did you know?
The seventh plague of Egypt was a storm of hailstones. The largest hailstones ever to have been recorded were the size of bowling balls. They fell in Kansas and weighed an incredible 1 lb 11 oz (760 g)!

Shortbread crunch

Cut up your squashed fly cookies and place them on a wire rack to cool. You can store the shortbread in an airtight container to keep it crisp and fresh.

BETHLEHEM STAR COOKIES

You will need

Measuring cup • Wooden spoon
Strainer • Saucepan • Rolling pin
Waxed paper • 2 baking sheets
Mixing bowl • Wire cooling rack
Large and small star cookie cutters
Skewer • Cutting board
Pastry brush • Thin colored ribbon

Ingredients for 20 cookies

¹/₄ cup (55 g)
butter

¹/₄ cup (50 ml)
pancake syrup

¹/₄ cup (55 g)
granulated sugar

1 cup (115 g)
cake flour

¹/₂ teaspoon
baking soda

¹/₂ teaspoon
cinnamon

¹/₂ teaspoon
allspice

10 fruit-flavored
hard candies

Confectioner's
gold dust, optional

H ang these spicy star cookies on your Christmas tree and watch the light twinkle through their pretty "stained-glass" centers. Turn the page to find out how to display these festive, edible decorations.

Making the cookies

1 Line the baking sheets with waxed paper. Sift the flour into a bowl. Add the sugar, spices, and baking soda.

2 Preheat the oven to 350°F/ 180°C. Warm the syrup and butter in a pan over a low heat. Stir until melted.

3 Pour the mixture into the bowl with the dry ingredients. Mix into a dough. Work the dough into a smooth ball with your hands.

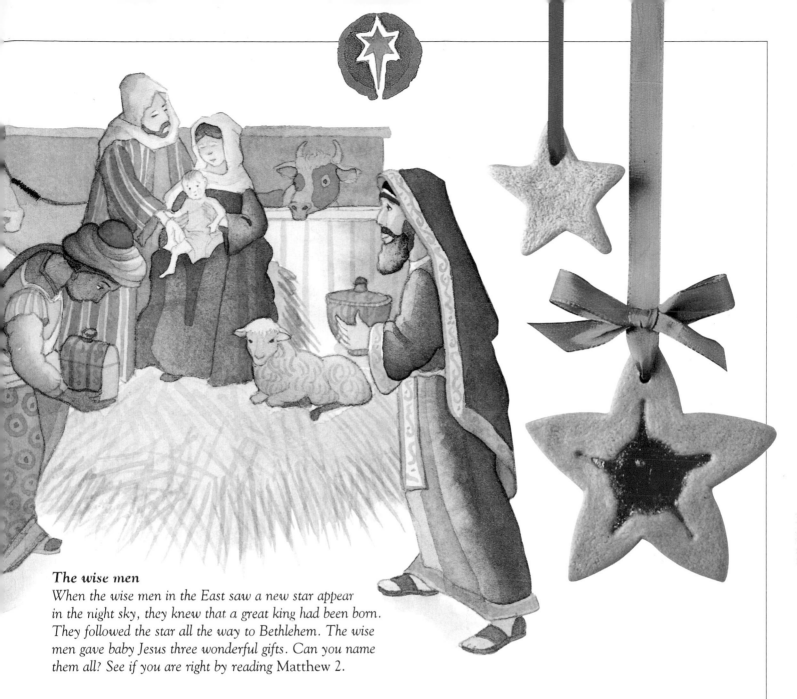

The wise men

When the wise men in the East saw a new star appear in the night sky, they knew that a great king had been born. They followed the star all the way to Bethlehem. The wise men gave baby Jesus three wonderful gifts. Can you name them all? See if you are right by reading Matthew 2.

4 Dust the work surface with flour. Roll out the cookie dough until it's ¼ in (5 mm) thick. Use the large star cutter to cut out ten cookies.

5 Place the stars on the baking sheets. Use the small star cutter to cut out the center of each cookie. Put a hard candy in each hole.

6 Bake the cookies for 10 minutes until golden brown. When the melted candies have hardened, place the cookies on a wire rack to cool.

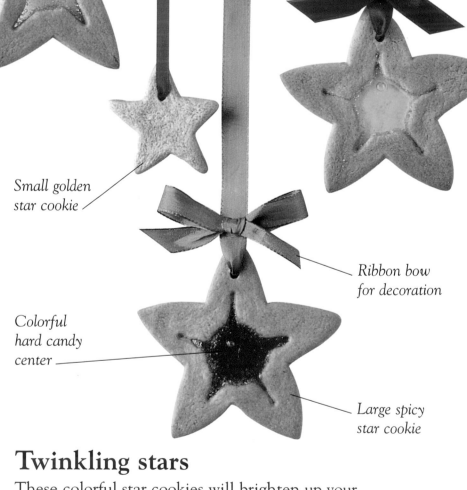

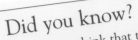

Did you know?
Some scientists think that the large star the wise men followed may have been Halley's comet, which was first seen in ancient times. Others believe that the star was a supernova – a faint star that suddenly explodes and becomes brighter. Chinese astronomers did record the appearance of such a star around the time of Jesus' birth.

Hanging the cookies

1 Use a skewer to make a hole through one point of each star. Rub gold dust on to the small stars with your finger.

2 Carefully thread a length of thin ribbon through each hole and tie into loops. Hang your stars as Christmas decorations.

Small golden star cookie

Ribbon bow for decoration

Colorful hard candy center

Large spicy star cookie

Twinkling stars

These colorful star cookies will brighten up your Christmas tree and make perfect gifts for visitors. Keep your cookies fresh in an airtight container until they are ready to put on the tree or eat.